5

Monkey got to work.
He twisted the leaves
and made Lion a crown.

But the wind blew it away.

Before long, Lion saw Zebra
eating her lunch.

"Zebra," roared Lion.

"Make me a crown of fruit."

So Zebra picked a melon.

She put on some berries

and made Lion a crown.

But it rotted in the hot sun.

Then Lion saw Hippo
taking a bath in the pool.

"Hippo!" roared Lion.

"Make me a crown of mud."

So Hippo patted and pulled the mud
until it looked like a crown.

But it started to rain.

Lion was sad.

He lay down under a tree.

Drip. Drip.

Something was falling onto his nose.

Drip. Drip.

It was sap. It was very sticky ...

... and it was making his nose itch.

Lion sneezed.

Achoo!

He sneezed again and again
and again.

Achoo! Achoo! Achoo!

His hair stood on end

and then it went hard.

Now Lion was happy.

He looked like a king.

Everyone came to look

at Lion's crown.

"I am a king!" he roared.

Story order

Look at these 5 pictures and captions.
Put the pictures in the right order
to retell the story.

1

The sap dripped on Lion's head.

2

The crown blew away.

3

Lion sneezed and sneezed.

4

Lion's hair stuck up in the air.

5

Zebra made a crown for Lion.

Independent Reading

This series is designed to provide an opportunity for your child to read on their own. These notes are written for you to help your child choose a book and to read it independently.

In school, your child's teacher will often be using reading books which have been banded to support the process of learning to read. Use the book band colour your child is reading in school to help you make a good choice. A Crown for Lion is a good choice for children reading at Orange Band in their classroom to read independently.

The aim of independent reading is to read this book with ease, so that your child enjoys the story and relates it to their own experiences.

About the book

Lion wants a crown to show that he is the king of the jungle. He orders the animals to make him a crown, but things keep going wrong. Then sap from the tree drips on Lion and he starts to sneeze ...

Before reading

Help your child to learn how to make good choices by asking:
"Why did you choose this book? Why do you think you will enjoy it?"
Look at the cover together and ask: "What do you think the story will be about?" Ask your child to think of what they already know about the story context. Then ask your child to read the title aloud.
Ask: "What do you know about lions in stories?"
Remind your child that they can sound out the letters to make a word if they get stuck.
Decide together whether your child will read the story independently or read it aloud to you.

During reading

Remind your child of what they know and what they can do independently. If reading aloud, support your child if they hesitate or ask for help by telling the word. If reading to themselves, remind your child that they can come and ask for your help if stuck.

After reading

Support comprehension by asking your child to tell you about the story. Use the story order puzzle to encourage your child to retell the story in the right sequence, in their own words. The correct sequence can be found on the next page.

Help your child think about the messages in the book that go beyond the story and ask: "Do you think the other animals like Lion? Why/why not?"

Give your child a chance to respond to the story: "Did you have a favourite part? Which crown do you think suits Lion best?"

Extending learning

Help your child understand the story structure by using the same sentence patterning and adding different elements. "Let's make up a new story about Lion. What else might Lion like, to show that he is a king? Perhaps he would like a gown or a throne? How will the other animals make it? What might go wrong?"

In the classroom, your child's teacher may be teaching adding the suffix -ed to the end of verbs, to make the simple past tense.

There are many in this book that you could look at with your child: *wanted, roared, twisted, picked, rotted, patted, pulled, looked, started, sneezed.*

Franklin Watts
First published in Great Britain in 2017
by The Watts Publishing Group

Copyright © The Watts Publishing Group 2017

Series Editors: Jackie Hamley and Melanie Palmer
Series Advisors: Dr Sue Bodman and Glen Franklin
Series Designer: Peter Scoulding

A CIP catalogue record for this book is
available from the British Library.

ISBN 978 1 4451 5423 7 (hbk)
ISBN 978 1 4451 5424 4 (pbk)
ISBN 978 1 4451 6101 3 (library ebook)

Printed in China

Franklin Watts
An imprint of
Hachette Children's Group
Part of The Watts Publishing Group
Carmelite House
50 Victoria Embankment
London EC4Y 0DZ

An Hachette UK Company
www.hachette.co.uk

www.franklinwatts.co.uk

FSC
www.fsc.org
MIX
Paper from
responsible sources
FSC® C104740

Answer to Story order: 2, 5, 1, 3, 4